Quincy Rumpel
and the All-Day Breakfast

QUINCY RUMPEL

and the
All-Day Breakfast

Betty Waterton

A Groundwood Book

Douglas & McIntyre

VANCOUVER / TORONTO / BUFFALO

Copyright © 1996 by Betty Waterton

Groundwood Books/Douglas & McIntyre
585 Bloor Street West
Toronto, Ontario M6G 1K5

Distributed in the U.S. by Publishers Group West
4065 Hollis Street
Emeryville, CA 94608

The publisher gratefully acknowledges the assistance of the Canada
Council and the Ontario Arts Council.

Canadian Cataloguing in Publication Data

Waterton, Betty
Quincy Rumpel and the all-day breakfast
"A Groundwood book".
ISBN 0-88899-225-4
I. Title.

PS8595.A79Q83 1996   jC813'.54   C96-930100-6
PZ7.W37Qu 1996

Design by Michael Solomon
Cover illustration by Ted Nasmith
Printed and bound in Canada

Contents

The author would like to thank the Cultural Services Branch, Ministry of Small Business, Tourism and Culture, Province of British Columbia.

1

The Turning Point

When Mrs. Rumpel served 8-Can Chicken Casserole to her family one evening, none of them guessed what a turning point it would be in their lives.

"Mom, it's good!" cried her children.

"Finger-licking good!" said Mr. Rumpel, licking his fingers.

Mrs. Rumpel flushed happily. "Thank you. It's a new recipe I found on a soup can. It makes quite a lot, too. Anyone ready for more?"

"It's good," murmured Leah, the middle Rumpel, as she shoved a little pile of chicken cubes to one corner of her plate. "But I don't think I want any more."

"Don't worry about her, Mom," said Quincy, the oldest. "She's just gone vegetarian again."

"We shouldn't waste it," said Mrs. Rumpel. "And the freezer is already full of leftovers." She turned to the youngest of her three offspring. "Morris, how about you? That's only your third helping."

"I'm full up to my neck. Maybe you could give it to Roxy and Fireweed."

Leah sighed dramatically. "Doesn't this child know that horses are vegetarians?"

"Listen, everybody!" cried Quincy suddenly. "I've just had a terrific idea. Mom, you always make too much food, and sometimes it's quite good, even. Like tonight, for instance. *And*, Dad's been talking about making another room in the attic. Haven't you, Dad?"

"I think I did mention the idea. Once."

"*And*, our apple trees haven't made any money yet—"

"They haven't even made any apples," said Morris. "They're still smaller than I am."

Quincy nodded. "Exactly. *So*, what does that all tell you?"

Morris shrugged, and the others looked

puzzled. Finally Leah spoke up hopefully. "We should move back to Vancouver, maybe?"

"No! I just love it here in Cranberry Corners." Quincy jumped up, knocking her chair over backwards. "Don't you see? We should open a bed-and-breakfast place—Rumpel Bed and Breakfast!"

"Rumpel Bed and Breakfast...it does have a nice ring," said Mrs. Rumpel. "We could put an ad in the Yellow Pages..."

"And *National Geographic*," cried Leah. "People all over the world read *National Geographic*."

"I suppose it wouldn't take much to finish off the attic—a few sheets of plywood and a window or two..." Producing a pencil stub and the new telephone bill from his pocket, Mr. Rumpel began making a list.

"We could put a hanging basket of geraniums in the bathroom," said Leah. "And our avocado plants..."

"And we could put a little box outside the bathroom door," added Morris. "Make 'em pay to get in."

"Grow up, Morris," said Quincy. "You can't do that. *Bed and breakfast* includes bathroom privileges."

"Speaking of food," said Mrs. Rumpel. "We'll need a bigger teapot. And we'd better get more chickens. People like to have fresh farm eggs for breakfast."

"Mother, how could you!" cried Leah. "Not more chickens! The poor things are just like your little slaves, running around laying their eggs for you. It's so gross..."

But Mrs. Rumpel was not listening. "I wonder if we should serve dinner as well as breakfast? I don't suppose we have to..."

"No, we don't," said Mr. Rumpel, his pencil poised in mid air. "But we will. We Rumpels always go the extra mile. Rumpel Ranch Bed and Breakfast shall become famous for its gastronomic delights."

"I suppose I could make my pineapple upside-down cake with maraschino cherries," murmured Mrs. Rumpel. "Everybody always likes that."

"Right on!" cried Quincy. "*And* we could

serve breakfast all day! That would be special. Why, we'll be so popular that we might have to fix up the old bat house and rent it out, too."

"You couldn't pay me to stay in the old bat house," said Leah.

"I wouldn't mind," said Morris. "But not all by myself."

"What are they talking about?" Mrs. Rumpel asked her husband.

"I think they mean the old homestead down in the hollow behind the barn. It used to belong to someone named *Batt*."

"But it's just a ruin. No one has lived there for ages."

"Don't worry. We won't involve it in our bed-and-breakfast business. I'll have my hands full fixing up the attic. I'll have to build proper stairs, to start with."

"Actually, Dad, I've just had another idea," cried Quincy. "Leah and I could move up to the attic for the time being. Then you could use our room for the guests. We could open the B and B right away."

"My goodness," said Mrs. Rumpel. "You

are full of ideas today, Quincy."

"I know," said Quincy. "Some days I'm like that."

2

A Beehive

Rumpel Ranch became a beehive of activity.

First a brochure was designed. After much discussion, it was decided to feature a photo of the five Rumpels standing on the lawn in front of the stately Empress Hotel in Victoria. "It's the best one we have," said Mrs. Rumpel. "We're all smiling." Under the photo were the words *Join the Rumpels for Luxurious Rooms, Exquisite Meals and Exciting Trail Rides at* RUMPEL BED AND BREAKFAST. *Breakfast Served All Day!*

After being photocopied in Cranberry Corners, the brochures were mailed out to everyone on the Rumpels' Christmas card list, plus a few others.

Leah and Quincy cleaned out their old room, and in the process discovered several long-lost items, including Leah's gym shorts, Quincy's bear-paw slippers and Snowflake's dog brush.

They lugged their clothes, books, jewellery and hair bows (Leah's), stuffed animals and soccer boots (Quincy's), up the ladder to their new quarters in the attic, along with Leah's posters of kittens, dogs and horses and Quincy's posters of dogs, horses and cowboys. Then Mrs. Rumpel, armed with the vacuum cleaner, advanced into their vacated room.

Eventually the grass was cut, the nasturtiums weeded, curtains washed and windows polished. Cushion covers were whipped off, laundered and reinstalled.

"I think Mom meant us to sew these back on," said Leah one day, as she pinned a blue velvet cover onto a cushion.

"Safety pins are one of the great inventions of the modern age," said Quincy. "We might as well use 'em. Where is Mom, anyway?"

"Upstairs, making lampshades. She read about how to make these really neat ones out of old jeans. They're supposed to look homey."

"Yikes! I hope she's not using my Prairie Wranglers. They're just starting to fit!" Dropping her half-pinned cushion, Quincy bounded towards the stairs and took them two at a time. Leah scurried after her.

They found their mother hunched over Grandma Rumpel's old sewing machine in the upstairs hall. She was muttering to herself. On the floor, among discarded zippers, pockets and waistbands, were three naked wire lampshade frames and a stack of denim squares.

"You didn't use my Prairie Wranglers, did you?" cried Quincy.

"I don't know," said Mrs. Rumpel crossly. "And I really don't care. My bobbin ran out before I even got started. Then the needle broke, and now I can't get this stupid new one threaded."

"You should wear your glasses more, Mom," said Leah. While she took over the needle-threading, Quincy checked out the dismembered jeans.

"Boy, that was lucky," she said, sitting down on the top step. "These are mostly Leah's...Mom, you need a new machine. They're computerized now, you know."

"No! No more sewing machines. When this one goes, sewing ends forever in this house."

With her equipment back in operation, Mrs. Rumpel began her attack on the denim squares. "I think these are going to look quite smart," she said as she held up the first finished lampshade. "Especially when I get the tassels on."

"Tassels?" Quincy looked at her in amazement. "Boy, that sounds like work—sewing on all those little balls."

"They come on a strip. I once trimmed some pyjamas with them for you when you were small. You loved those pyjamas."

"Huh." Quincy looked around. "So where are they? The tassels for the lampshades, I mean."

"Dad and Morris are picking them up for me while they're in town. I told them to get navy blue."

"What did they go to town for this time?" asked Leah.

"I don't honestly know. They seem to keep running out of things for the renovations."

"I'll just be glad when Dad gets the stairs to the attic made," said Quincy. "It's a pain using that ladder and trapdoor all the time, especially when you're carrying a bunch of food. Like last night, for instance, the orange juice slurped out and practically wrecked our popcorn and grilled cheese sandwiches."

Mrs. Rumpel continued her sewing, her machine quivering ominously. "It's more important that we get our guest accommodation in order, and your old room needed a few repairs," she said. "Remember our motto— *Luxurious Rooms, Exquisite Meals and Exciting Trail Rides*."

"That's not quite honest, you know," said Quincy. "We've only got my horse—Roxy."

"Don't forget Fireweed," said Leah.

"Too old. Way, way, too old."

"He's only twenty-two. Lots of horses live longer than that."

"I know that. Did you think I didn't know that?"

"Girls! Stop arguing. People can bring their own horses," snapped Mrs. Rumpel, whose latest lampshade did not seem to be fitting.

Just then the scrunch of tires on the driveway below signalled the return of Mr. Rumpel and Morris.

"Here come your tassels, Mom," announced Leah.

"They'd better be navy blue," said Mrs. Rumpel grimly.

3

A New Chicken Window

"Tassels?" Mr. Rumpel looked surprised. "Actually, they kind of slipped my mind. We were pretty busy, you know."

"Man," said Morris. "You should have seen the sale at the hardware store! Dad got four snow shovels. They were so cheap. We got some wallpaper with ducks on it, too, and wait till you see the red plastic window we got for the chicken house. It's just beautiful!"

As Morris hurried out to the chicken house after his father, Mrs. Rumpel called after them, "But my tassels! I really need those tassels..."

"And our stairs. When are you going to make our stairs?" cried Leah and Quincy.

"Tomorrow. We'll do everything tomorrow. Don't worry."

An hour and a half later, everyone was

summoned outside to admire the new chicken window. That was when the phone rang.

"I'll get it!" hollered Morris. After a few minutes, he came flying out of the house.

"A customer!" he yelled, skidding to a stop in front of the chicken house. "We've got a customer, and I'll bet you'll never guess who it is!"

"Princess Diana?" Leah ventured hopefully.

"Don't be silly," said Quincy. "Who is it, Morris? Wayne Gretzky or somebody?"

"I did send a few brochures to Ottawa," said Mrs. Rumpel. "You never know..."

"Aunt Fan!" shouted Morris. "Aunt Fan is back from her cruise and she's driving out here in her Land Rover and she's bringing some friends she met on the cruise and they're getting here tomorrow!"

"Well!" said Mr. Rumpel. "It seems we're in business!"

A glazed look came over Mrs. Rumpel's eyes. "Food," she murmured. "We'll need food. And the tassels aren't on, and the guest bed isn't made up yet and the fridge needs defrosting and..."

"Don't worry, Mom," said Quincy, as they made their way back to the house. "I'll go to town with Dad tomorrow and get the groceries for you. You just stay home and take it easy. You'll have Leah and Morris to help you."

"I thought I'd do a nice painting for the dining room," said Leah. "It needs sprucing up. Maybe a picture of a moose standing in Cranberry Lake..."

"I have to check out my red wrigglers tomorrow," said Morris. "I think I'll do it in the bathtub."

"You are not going to put those worms in our bathtub," said Mrs. Rumpel. Then she gave a little gasp. "With more people coming, we're going to need your room, too, Morris. You'll have to move out to your tree house, and soon."

"Oh, *man*!"

"Stop groaning," said his mother. "Your room is going to need a major overhaul if Aunt Fan is going to sleep in it."

"Well, if it's just Aunt Fan, at least I won't

need to move out my red wrigglers."

"Morris," said Quincy. "Sometimes I think you are intellectually challenged, for sure."

4

The Shopping Trip

The Cranberry Corners Megamarket was crowded.

As Quincy steered her wobbling cart down the crowded aisle, she felt something ram into the back of her knees.

"Uh-oh," said a small voice.

Quincy whirled around. A small figure in purple shorts and a Lion King T-shirt hurriedly backed up her mini shopping cart.

"Who let you loose in here, Crocus McAddams?" asked Quincy, rubbing the back of her legs. "Where's your mother?"

For a moment Crocus stared up, her blue eyes wide. Then she opened her mouth. "MOMMY!" she screeched. "MOMMY! MOMMY!"

"What's the matter, little girl?" asked a passing shopper, glaring at Quincy. "Is somebody being mean to you?"

Suddenly the aisle was clogged with shopping carts, as grownups clustered protectively around Crocus. They were all staring at Quincy.

"I didn't do anything!" she protested. "This is Crocus McAddams. She lives next door to us, sort of. Tell them, Crocus. Tell them who I am."

Crocus gazed up at all the concerned faces. Not for a long time had she been the centre of so much attention. Giving a quivering sigh, she shook her head silently and managed to squeeze out two tears.

Just then a voice rang out from somewhere among the vegetables. "Crocus! Where are you, Crocus?" And a moment later, Loralee McAddams was making her way towards them.

"So, Quincy. How are you? How is the new bed-and-breakfast business going?"

"Really great, Loralee. That's why we had to come in to buy some groceries. We've got customers already."

"So soon? But that's wonderful. Your publicity campaign must have paid off."

"It's only Aunt Fan, but she's bringing

some friends she met on her cruise."

"My goodness. From her cruise? They'll have been having really elegant meals, then. I hope your mother is planning something special."

"Oh, she is. Tonight we're having roast moose and Yorkshire pudding. I'm just trying to find a Yorkshire pudding mix..."

"Hmmm." Loralee handed Crocus a banana to peel. "You must give them something more exotic than that. Let me think. How about a baked vegetable frittata accompanied by a marinated fresh pea and onion salad...and some stir-fried broccoli with black bean sauce?"

Quincy shook her head. "I don't think so. Dad hates broccoli, and Mom has the moose all thawed out."

"Well, then at least do something gourmet with the moose. Yes, curried moose and rice might be all right, but you must get some popadams to go with it. They'll help to make the meal more interesting. Actually, I could come over and give your mother a hand with dinner tonight..."

Quincy watched their neighbour as she sashayed away with Crocus in tow.

In her T-shirt and jeans and gold hoop earrings, and with her long black hair hanging loose, Loralee McAddams hardly looks like the mother of three weird little kids, thought Quincy. *Mom has three kids, too, but when she goes grocery shopping, she wears sweats and runners and the plastic straw necklace Morris made her in kindergarten.*

Mr. Rumpel was waiting by the check-out. He was easy to spot in his new John Deere tractor cap and striped overalls.

"Great Scott!" he exclaimed when he saw Quincy's cart. "What's with all the rice?"

"I didn't know if Mom had any or not. I met Loralee, and she says we should have some tonight for our customers. I think she's coming over to help Mom make dinner more interesting."

"Oh, boy," sighed Mr. Rumpel. "Quincy, you'd better go and get a few cans of pork and beans..."

5

Popadams

"Thank goodness Aunt Fan isn't here yet," said Quincy, as their brown station wagon pulled up in front of Rumpel Ranch. "I've absolutely *got* to wash my hair before anyone sees me."

Mrs. Rumpel was standing at the front door in her shiny black-and-white cow apron. "I hope you remembered the tassels," she said.

Quincy groaned.

Mr. Rumpel grunted as he heaved a sack of rice onto his shoulder. "Didn't have time. Please send Morris or Leah out to help with this stuff..."

"Morris is still busy moving out of his room, and Leah is upstairs crying. She thinks the moose in her painting isn't quite right. I told her it looks just fine, but she says I don't understand about art. What's all that rice for?

And this big bag of peanuts?"

"I met Loralee in the Megamarket," said Quincy, "and she says we should really have something gourmet for dinner, what with Aunt Fan and her friends just back from a cruise and all. Anyway, I couldn't find any Yorkshire pudding mix. And everybody loves peanuts. We can put them in little dishes all over the house."

As Quincy staggered into the kitchen with the second sack of rice, she bumped into Morris's rear end, which was protruding out of the refrigerator.

"Get out of my way," she yelled, heaving the rice onto a chair. "Why aren't you out helping us with this stuff?"

"I'm thinking." Morris's voice was muffled, coming from the interior of the refrigerator. "I'm thinking about where to put my red wrigglers. Can I put them up in the attic with you? They don't make any noise."

"No! Take them out to the tree house. They'll love it up there."

"No, they won't. They're scared of birds."

"Just get them out of the bathroom," ordered his mother, as she unpacked a bag of groceries. She held up an unfamiliar package and waved it at Quincy. "What on earth is this?"

"Popadams. Loralee says we just have to have them with the curry, they're so totally good."

Equipped with several new bottles of shampoo, conditioner and bubble bath, Quincy had almost made it out of the kitchen when Mrs. Rumpel called out, "Come back here. I need help putting this food away."

"But, Mom, Loralee's coming over to help you, and my hair is an absolute schmozz." Taking the band off her ponytail, Quincy shook out her red hair. "See? It's all stringy and limp, and with Aunt Fan's fancy friends coming..."

Mrs. Rumpel sighed. "It doesn't look so bad to me. But go, if you must. Just don't use the new soap—and clean out the tub afterwards."

As Quincy ran up the stairs, she encountered a strong smell of turpentine coming from her parents' room. She poked her head in the door. Leah was ferociously jabbing a brush at a painting propped up on the dresser.

Wisps of blonde hair peeked out from under her flowered head scarf. She wore an old paint-splattered shirt of her father's that reached down to her knees, and her face was daubed with paint and tears.

But she still manages to look sort of perky, thought Quincy grudgingly. "How come you're messing up Mom and Dad's room?"

"You didn't expect me to lug all this stuff up that dumb ladder into the attic, did you? Oh, Quince, Morris says it doesn't look like a moose at all. He says it looks like a hippopotamus with antlers."

Quincy squinted at the large brown creature with its big nose and soulful eyes and a water-lily hanging out of its mouth. It was standing knee-deep in bright-green water. "Hmmm. Maybe it's his legs. They're sort of a teensy bit fat for a moose, maybe. But he's got a nice expression. And do you think maybe the water should be murkier? Cranberry Lake isn't all that green, usually."

"It's green because of that darned old picture underneath—the one we found at the bat house once. Artists paint over old canvases all the time, but this dumb green keeps showing through."

"Huh. Well, it looks pretty good anyway. Don't worry about what Morris says. Anyway, I think Mom's getting kind of twitchy. Maybe you'd better go down."

Armed with her toiletries, Quincy disappeared into the bathroom and locked the door. An hour later, when she emerged in a cloud of raspberry-smelling steam, all traces of Leah and her moose were gone.

6

Twinkles

In her freshly laundered Prairie Wrangler jeans and western shirt with the pearl snaps, Quincy ducked into her parents' room. Standing in front of the full-length mirror, she studied her reflection.

Not too bad, she thought, after removing the congealed clump of doggy treats that was making an unattractive bulge in her hip pocket. *And that new shampoo is the best yet. My hair looks positively thick.*

Proceeding downstairs, she found Leah's moose hanging in the dining room, its legs now looking somewhat spindly. On the sideboard sat the Rumpels' newly polished silver tea service. On either side of it stood two ceramic elephants holding green candles in their upraised trunks. The elephants—sort of a mottled pink colour—had been made by

Mrs. Rumpel in a long-ago ceramics class.

Studying the whole arrangement with a worried frown was Mrs. Rumpel herself.

"Oh, I love those elephants, Mom. They've got real personality. We should use them all the time. But I don't know about *green* candles..."

Mrs. Rumpel plucked the green candles from their holders and replaced them with red ones.

"Not red, Mom. Too Christmas-y. Haven't you got any other colours? Like maybe blue? Blue would look nice."

"No blue. I've only got red and green," said Mrs. Rumpel, as she snatched the red candles from the elephants' trunks and jammed in the green ones again.

"I guess green is okay. Hey! Something smells like hot oil!"

Picking up her trailing pineapple-patterned muu-muu (sent from Hawaii last year by Aunt Fan), Mrs. Rumpel headed for the kitchen after Quincy.

There, in the swirling vapours above the

stove, hovered a phantom-like figure in orange harem pants. It appeared to be scooping things out of a pot.

Quincy stared at their neighbour in her gauzy blouse, gold vest and jangling bracelets, her dark hair hanging over her shoulder in a single thick braid.

"Wow, Loralee. You look so...different. Sort of exotic, almost. Are those the popadams?"

Loralee's braid bobbed up and down in assent as she retrieved another one from the pot.

"Are you sure they're all right?" asked Mrs. Rumpel, looking at the growing pile of limp pancake-like objects.

"They'll probably crisp up soon," said Loralee. "Maybe I took them out too early. I've never actually made them before."

"Why don't you stay and help us eat them?" asked Quincy.

"I don't want to intrude or anything," said Loralee. "But I would just *love* to meet your guests and hear all about their cruise. I've always wanted to go on a Caribbean cruise."

"It wasn't a Caribbean cruise," said Mrs. Rumpel. "It was a St. Lawrence River cruise."

"Aunt Fan sent us a postcard from Rimouski."

Just as Quincy was saying this, there was a knock at the front door.

"Oh, they can't be here already!" cried Mrs. Rumpel, straightening her muu-muu and looking aghast at Quincy. "Where's your father?"

"Helping Morris, I guess." Fluffing out her hair and smiling a bright welcome, Quincy sprinted for the door and flung it open.

There, dressed in a purple party dress and mismatched socks, and clutching a large, grumpy-looking grey cat, stood Crocus.

"Your doorbell is too high," she said, frowning at Quincy.

"You could have come in the back door, you know, Crocus. What do you want?"

Wandering into the living room, Crocus gazed around vaguely. "I have to ask Mommy something."

"Crocus, is that you?" asked Loralee, poking her head out of the kitchen. "What are you doing here? Is something the matter? Where's Poppy? She's supposed to be looking after you till Daddy gets home."

"She's busy. She's doing a hard jigsaw puzzle."

"So. What do you want?"

"Um, Mommy...is Twinkles a boy or a girl?"

"Crocus, we're very busy here. You know very well Twinkles is a boy. Now run on back home."

"I'm too tired." As Crocus sagged dramatically onto a footstool, Twinkles leaped out of her arms and disappeared.

"Get that cat out of here," ordered Mrs. Rumpel. "Remember Aunt Fan's allergy."

Just then a voice sang out from the top of the stairs. "I hear voices. Is Aunt Fan here? I'm just on my way down..." It was Leah, wearing a long crocheted granny-square jumper and floppy velvet hat. ".....EEEEEEK! A raccoon!" she cried, as something grey and furry streaked past her.

Suddenly they heard a whooping sound outside. "YO! YO! YAHOO!"

"Coyotes?" wondered Loralee.

"Probably Morris," said Mrs. Rumpel.

"No, it's not," said Quincy. "That's Dad."

Everyone rushed outside. There, in the tree house high up in the big cottonwood, two figures were wildly waving their arms and shouting.

"Come down at once, Harvey," said Mrs. Rumpel. "Aunt Fan will be here any minute and Twinkles is loose!"

"Put the ladder back! Put the ladder back!" yelled Mr. Rumpel, pointing to the ground where a long wooden ladder lay beside the inert body of the Rumpels' dog, Snowflake.

"Oh, poor Snowflake. Did the ladder fall on our poor puppy?" Tripping over her granny squares, Leah rushed towards the big white, dazed-looking animal.

"Snowflake almost made it up the ladder," said Morris. "But not quite."

"Put it back!" ordered Mr. Rumpel. "We want to come down."

The ground crew almost had the ladder in position, when they heard a musical *beep-beep-ba-ba-beep* coming from the driveway.

"That's 'O Canada'!" cried Quincy. "Aunt Fan is here!"

7

Honk If You Love Beavers

Once again the ladder clattered to the ground as Quincy, Leah, Loralee and Mrs. Rumpel hurried after the speeding Crocus to the front of the house.

There an ancient Land Rover was grinding to a dusty stop, the maple leaf flag on its antenna still fluttering and its horn still tootling out "O Canada."

"Look! Aunt Fan's got a new bumper sticker," said Quincy. "HONK IF YOU LOVE BEAVERS."

The driver's door swung open and a tall, thin figure emerged, clad in wrinkled knee-length khaki shorts and belted safari jacket. "Here we are, Rumpels," announced Aunt Fan. "I hope you have something to eat, Rose. We're famished. Quincy, have you been colouring your hair? It seems different. And those harem trousers are a mite skimpy, dear."

"That's not me, Aunt Fan. That's Loralee McAddams, our neighbour."

Wisps of orange-red hair straggled out from under Aunt Fan's Desert Storm-style hat as she advanced upon the little group and proceeded to hug each one in turn. "Where's Harvey?" she asked, when she reached the end of the line. "And I don't see little Boris."

"Morris, Aunt Fan," said Mrs. Rumpel. "And he's not so little any more. He's almost up to my shoulder now, you know."

The other four occupants of the Land Rover climbed out and lined themselves up beside it in a neat row. Quincy studied them carefully. One of the large ones—the one with the beard—wore a green business suit. The other was tall and blonde, in shiny green tights and matching leather jacket. The two small ones were dressed identically in short pants, green knee socks, white sweaters with HARVARD on them, and new TYRRELL MUSEUM ball caps—one red, one blue.

Morris would die for one of those caps, thought Quincy.

"These are the Bagels," Aunt Fan was saying. "The two small ones are called Jason and Mason, I think."

"That's Justin and Dustin," said Mrs. Bagel. "Our munchkins. They're twins. Boys, why are you making those faces?"

"That little kid's socks don't match, Ma. And now look. She's sticking out her tongue at us!"

Suddenly Crocus, protesting loudly, was propelled into the house by her mother.

"Say something, Mom," Quincy whispered to Mrs. Rumpel. "Say *Welcome to Rumpel Ranch,* or something."

"Welcome to Wumpel..." began Mrs. Rumpel nervously, only to be interrupted by a plaintive "HALLOOOO!" from the tree house.

"Wolves!" cried Mr. Bagel. "Take shelter, everybody!"

In due time, Mr. Rumpel and Morris were

released from their perch in the cottonwood tree, and they joined the others.

There was plenty of rice and curried moose for dinner, and as no one had ever had popadams before—limp or crisp—Mrs. Rumpel felt that the meal was not only reasonably successful, but even rather gourmet.

On one of their trips to the kitchen to fetch a cheese ball for the Bagels, Leah remarked to Quincy, "They don't talk very much, do they?"

"They don't get much chance, with Aunt Fan."

"And why did Mom send us out here to get funny things like this, anyway? We haven't got a cheese ball. I've never even seen a cheese ball."

"I know. Mom just didn't want to admit we don't have that kind of stuff. But I'll bet we could make one..."

Rolling up her sleeves, Quincy got busy. But when she tried to sculpt Cheez Whiz and Worcestershire sauce on the bread board, she groaned. "I don't think this is going to work.

It needs a stiffener..."

"How about crushed Cheerios and Shredded Wheat?" suggested Leah.

"Good thinking!" And so, fortified, pummelled and rolled in Shredded Wheat, the cheesy concoction was at last delivered to the dining room on a platter, surrounded by soda biscuits.

"A hedgehog!" squealed Dustin and Justin in unison, and they disappeared under the table.

As Mrs. Rumpel wondered how to serve Loralee's rapidly collapsing strawberry pavlova, Aunt Fan gave everyone a running commentary about the birds she had seen on their recent cruise.

"I never expected to see rufous-sided towhees on the St. Lawrence, but I did. Not many, to be sure, but some. And would you believe a black-bellied plover?"

On their next trip to the kitchen to hunt for slivered almonds to sprinkle on their guests' dessert, Leah said to Quincy, "Did you see the way the Bagels kept looking at my moose picture? I think they were impressed."

"I think they were looking at Mom's candlesticks. They're pretty unique, you know...I can't find any slivered almonds. Here. Chop up some peanuts."

"And how was your trip out from Toronto?" Mrs. Rumpel was asking their guests. "Aunt Fan says you all went to the big dinosaur museum in Alberta. That must have been fantastic."

"It was frightfully crowded," said Mrs. Bagel.

"They had huge dinosaur eggs," said Justin. "As big as houses."

"No, they weren't," said Dustin. "They were small—as small as peas."

"No dinosaur eggs are as small as peas," said Morris. "Or as big as houses. The biggest eggs ever found were about as big as soccer balls, but kind of lumpy. They were probably from hypselosauruses. Some eggs are more like chicken eggs. But, of course, the eggs of the protoceratops are bigger than that. For instance, at Egg Mountain, Montana..."

Oh, no, thought Quincy. *If there is one thing Morris knows, it's dinosaurs. He'll go on for hours!* She looked around the table at their guests.

Poor Mr. Bagel. He's all red in the face. He's fanning himself and wiping his forehead with his serviette. And Mrs. Bagel has gone all pale. I think she's taking the peanuts out of her pavlova! Justin and Dustin have disappeared under the table again! And just look at Aunt Fan. She's actually fiddling with her silverware!

Finally Mrs. Rumpel said, "I don't think anyone wants to hear any more about dinosaur eggs, Morris."

You've sure got that right, Mom, thought Quincy.

"But I never got to tell them about the nests..." grumbled Morris, as he subsided into a grumpy silence.

8

Red Wrigglers

As soon as dinner was over, Mr. Rumpel went to hunt for his doorknob collection to show to Mr. Bagel. Meanwhile, Mr. and Mrs. Bagel wandered around the dining room inspecting the knick-knacks. Mrs. Bagel seemed particularly intrigued by the elephant candlesticks. Picking one up, she studied it carefully. "Very interesting," she said. "Are these old?"

"Really old," Quincy told her. "Mom made them before Morris was born."

"We had trouble with the firing that day," said Mrs. Rumpel, blushing happily at this unexpected attention. "That's why they're sort of blotchy. But all in all, they didn't turn out too badly, did they?" Mrs. Bagel didn't answer.

Suddenly the front door flew open and

Justin and Dustin burst in. They were howling mightily and covered in dust. Right behind them stalked Crocus. Her purple party dress was grimy, and her blue eyes flashed dangerously.

"Munchkins! What happened?" cried Mrs. Bagel, as the twins cowered behind her legs.

"Crocus decked 'em," chuckled Morris, who was bringing up the rear. "They were making fun of her socks again, so she decked 'em."

"Say good-night, Crocus," said Loralee, grabbing her by her sash. "We're going home."

By ten o'clock, peace and quiet had almost descended on Rumpel Ranch. Morris had retired to the tree house, Aunt Fan to the chesterfield, and the others to their various bedrooms.

Up in the attic, Quincy was sitting on the edge of her bed, tugging at her jeans. At last she managed to kick them off, sending them flying halfway across the room, where they landed on Leah's bed.

Leah chucked them back. "Quince, I wish you wouldn't do that all the time. It's getting tiresome."

"It's part of my exercise program. It builds up my riding muscles."

Taking off her velvet hat, Leah placed it carefully on her pink papier-mâché hatstand, which she'd moulded from an inflated balloon. Then, just as she was about to turn out the light, there was an unearthly scream downstairs.

Quincy sat bolt upright in her bed. "Whazzat?"

They heard excited voices, the sound of bedroom doors opening and closing, and then some loud sneezing from the living room.

Sliding out of bed, Quincy made her way to the trap door. Lying on her stomach, she hung over it, listening.

"It was just Twinkles," she reported. "He was hiding under the blankets on Mrs. Bagel's bed. He must have surprised her. Then he went downstairs. I think Dad's throwing him out now."

Once again things were quiet, and both girls were soon asleep.

In the middle of the night, Quincy was wakened by the smell of chocolate.

A small figure in wrinkled hockey pyjamas was standing by her bed, waving a wobbling flashlight around.

"Morris! What are you doing? For Pete's sake, I thought we'd have some privacy when we moved up here. Why aren't you in the tree house?"

Morris stuffed the last of an Oreo cookie into his mouth. "I can't find my red wrigglers."

"Well, they'd sure better not be in here, I'll tell you that."

"But they're part of my science project. They're making compost. And Mom won't let me keep them under the sink."

"I don't blame her. Anyway, you should have them in a proper worm composting bin, not an ice-cream bucket. Now go on back to your tree house."

"Quincy, it's dark up in the tree, and there are funny noises. Can't I stay here?"

Quincy groaned. "I suppose so. But stop waving that flashlight around. Put Leah's sleeping bag on the floor over there in the corner and use that." Pulling the quilt over her head, Quincy went back to sleep.

Rumpel Ranch was finally quiet.

9

Early Breakfast

"Wake up, girls. I need you in the kitchen."

Quincy moaned and slowly opened one eye. The sky outside was faintly pink, but the attic room was still dark and shadowy. A head was poking up through the open trap door.

"Mom?"

"Yes," hissed the head. "Now wake up Leah and hurry downstairs."

"But it's not even daylight yet!"

"The Bagels may be early risers."

"But aren't we supposed to say what time breakfast is? Like ten o'clock, or something?"

"Not at Rumpel Bed and Breakfast. You know we serve breakfast all day. It was even your idea. So we may as well get started." With these words, the talking head vanished.

Eventually both girls were dressed and

making their careful way down the ladder. As they tiptoed past their former bedroom, Quincy whispered, "I *knew* the Bagels wouldn't be up yet! Mom is getting too up-tight about making meals. I'm worried about her."

"The terrible twins must still be asleep, too," said Leah. "I don't hear anything from their room, either."

"That's good, because there's no way I could face them this early in the day." But even as she spoke, Quincy's feet suddenly went from under her.

"WHOOOOPS!"

She skidded down the hall with a plastic ice-cream bucket rattling ahead of her, spilling out its contents.

"What on *earth*?!!" Sitting on the floor, Quincy lifted her hand and stared at it. A dark, gooey mess, some of it moving, coated her fingers.

"Worms!" gasped Leah. Hurtling past her sister, she plunged downstairs...neck-and-neck with the bucket.

The door of Morris's room opened cautiously and two pale faces peered out. Dustin and Justin were wearing identical *Phantom of the Opera* pyjamas, and their baseball caps.

They glared at Quincy. "We found an ice-cream pail under the bed, but it didn't have any ice cream in it," said Dustin. "It was just full of mud and worms. We put it out in the hall."

By this time Mrs. Rumpel, alerted by Leah, was on the scene in her rubber boots. "Quincy, get Morris to clean up this mess at once!" she ordered.

"Why me? Leah can call him. I have to have a shower now. I mean *really* have to!" And she ducked into the bathroom.

When she reappeared, she found her father scouring the hall floor. Morris's red wrigglers and their scattered ecosystem had been returned to the ice-cream pail, but Morris himself was still missing.

Not surprisingly, after all the commotion outside their door, the rest of the Bagels were now up. And hungry. Suddenly Mrs. Rumpel had many demands on her time—making porridge, mixing up pancakes, cooking sausages, scrambling eggs and chopping potatoes for hash-browns. Quincy and Leah and even Mr. Rumpel were pressed into service, and for a while Morris was forgotten.

Then, just as the four Bagels were confronting their bountiful breakfast, a haggard-looking, rumpled figure slumped past on its way to the kitchen.

"That's the last time I'll ever use Leah's sleeping bag," whined Morris, peering into the fridge. "It was so lumpy I couldn't even sleep."

"What were you doing with Leah's sleeping bag?" asked his mother. "I thought you were in the treehouse."

"Ha!" said Quincy. "Now I remember! Morris was scared, so he slept on the floor in our room last night. I forgot all about him."

"This is totally disgusting," cried Leah. "Nobody told me he was there! And I didn't say he could use my sleeping bag. I want a new one."

"Don't be silly," said Mrs. Rumpel. "I'll

put it through the wash for you, if you like."

"I do. I do. I'll go and get it right away. But first I have to take my collection out of it."

"Your collection? What collection?" asked Morris.

"My pink pig collection, of course. Dad hasn't put up a shelf for them yet, so that's where I keep them."

"Your pink pig collection? You mean I slept with five hundred *pink pigs*?"

"She's only got fifty-six," said Quincy. "Don't exaggerate."

10

A Good Idea

"They're looking at my painting again!" whispered Leah, peeking into the dining room. "The moose does look pretty good now, doesn't he?"

"Except he looks sort of like an ant-eater," said Morris. "His nose should be humpier."

"Since when did you become an expert on moose?" cried Leah.

"It's a very nice picture, dear. Very tranquil." It was Aunt Fan on her way into the kitchen, her head at a peculiar angle.

"Aunt Fan, what's the matter with your neck?" asked Quincy.

"I got a crick in it last night, sneezing so hard when that cat landed on me. That is one obnoxious cat, believe me. Where does your mother keep the aspirin?"

"On the top shelf," said Mrs. Rumpel,

scurrying past with yet another plate of pancakes for their guests. "Quincy, try and get that pancake batter off the wall. Justin and Dustin wanted their pancakes shaped like asteroids, would you believe, and most of it landed behind the stove."

Finally breakfast was over. Even Aunt Fan, with her head tilted to one side, had managed to eat a sizeable portion of oatmeal porridge, eggs, sausages, toast and yogurt.

When the Bagels at last staggered out of the dining room rubbing their stomachs, Mrs. Rumpel said to Quincy, "Go and get the hot water bottle for Aunt Fan. Leah, you start clearing the table, and Morris, you can load the dishwasher."

"Dishwasher, fishwater," muttered Morris. "What I want to know is when do I get my room back?"

"Soon, I'm afraid. Somehow I don't think the Bagels will be staying around long. They don't seem interested in doing anything much. They do want to see the barn, though."

"They probably expected to go trail riding," said Quincy, looking at her mother meaningfully.

"I didn't actually say *horse* trail riding," said Mrs. Rumpel. "*Come ride the trails* could mean bring your own bicycles."

"Mom, that's misleading advertising. Anyway, now that they're here, we've got to figure out something for them to do if we want them to stick around. Why don't we take them on a tour of our apple orchard and finish it off with a picnic lunch? A picnic would be easy to do—maybe some roast chickens and potato salad with a few pies. Lemon and apple would be nice."

"And later we could show them our slides of Niagara Falls!" said Leah.

"I am not preparing food for a picnic," said Mrs. Rumpel. "I've got lunch all planned."

"What about playing horseshoes?" wondered Morris. "Horseshoes are cool. I know where there are some, too. I'll go get 'em!" Before anyone could answer, he galloped away towards the barn.

"That's a good idea," said Aunt Fan. "I love quoits."

"Maybe we could have a tournament," said Mrs. Rumpel. "That might keep them happy for another day. Quincy, after you get the hot water bottle, find your father and tell him we need him, *tout de suite*."

Leah looked at her mother in surprise. "Your French is getting better, Mom."

"*Un peu*. I've been brushing up. After all, we did send a few brochures to Ottawa."

11

Body Language

Quincy drifted through the orchard, looking for her father. She was lost in
thought.

*The more I think about the Bagels, the more I
think we're wasting our time with horseshoes.
They're not the outdoorsy type. Mr. Bagel was real-
ly interested in Dad's doorknob collection. And Mrs.
Bagel seemed to like Mom's elephant candleholders.
Maybe they're antique dealers or something...*

Suddenly she was startled by a voice.
"What ho, Quincy!"

"Aunt Fan?"

"Over here, girl. I'm stuck in some bram-
bles." The voice was coming from a thicket
on the edge of the orchard.

Hurrying over, Quincy found her great-
aunt held prisoner in the thorny grip of mam-
moth blackberry vines. She was still in her

MacGregor plaid dressing gown. A hot water bottle was firmly tied to her neck with pantyhose, and a large pair of binoculars dangled on her chest.

"Aunt Fan! What are you doing out here?" cried Quincy, carefully pulling away some vines. "I thought you had gone to lie down."

"I heard a quail calling, and I simply had to see him. Great galaxies, but those little guys can run! There was a whole family of them, but they disappeared into this barbarous jungle and I couldn't extricate myself."

"I know. We wear overalls and tie on our hats when we pick berries."

After many mutterings, Aunt Fan was finally released.

"I'd better find Dad now if we're going to have this horseshoe tournament," said Quincy.

"Oh, don't bother your poor father. All we need is a couple of iron pegs and some horseshoes."

"Morris is getting the horseshoes, but we'll have to find some iron pegs somewhere— probably in the barn."

On the way they met Morris, just leaving. He was carrying an armful of old horseshoes of various sizes. "They were nailed up all over the place," he said. "And guess who was in there? The Bagels!"

"Mom said they wanted to see it," said Quincy.

"They were there all right. All four of 'em. And the goats. But I think they're scared of Lettuce. She was trying to eat Mrs. Bagel's leather jacket. They're still poking around in there."

As Morris staggered off with his horseshoes, Quincy turned to Aunt Fan. "I never thought Mrs. Bagel would like poking around in old barns. She really doesn't seem like the type."

"You never can tell about people. Sometimes they surprise you."

"I guess maybe you're right. Mom surprised me lately. She wrote 'Exciting Trail Rides' on our brochure, and that sounds as if we have a bunch of horses, which we don't. I didn't think that's right. Mom always used to be so honest..."

"There does appear to be a slight exaggeration there. Of course, some might call it poetic licence."

"I wouldn't."

Quincy pulled open one of the big barn doors and they stepped inside. The door swung closed behind them, shutting out the bright morning sunshine.

There was a smell of hay, horses and old leather. And silence.

"HALLOOO!" hollered Aunt Fan.

"They're not here. It's too quiet. Those kids had better not have touched my new western saddle..." Alarmed at this thought, Quincy darted into the tack room.

After examining her saddle carefully for fingerprints, Quincy relaxed. She gave it a little rub with a polishing cloth and suddenly burst into song: "Oh, give me land, lots of land, under starry skies above..."

"Is that you, Mrs. Bagel?" shouted a voice, and the barn door opened. It was Leah, standing in a shaft of sunlight.

"No, of course it isn't," said Quincy, appearing from the tack room. "It's me. Morris said they came in here, but they're not here now."

"Well, they've disappeared. Justin and Dustin were in the living room playing Trivial Pursuit—*adult* Trivial Pursuit! They said it challenges them. Then suddenly they weren't there any more. What a weird family. They don't talk much and they're always wearing all that green. Morris thinks they've all got sort of pointy ears, too."

"I've noticed that. Not so much their ears, but the way they act. I guess you'd call it body language. It can be very important. Like, they don't lean forward when they're talking to you. They sort of lean away. And their eyes are always darting around."

Leah nodded. "And the way Dustin and Justin are always chewing that green gum! Quince, I'm worried about Mom's body language. She is really banging things around in the kitchen this morning. I think it's because of the cow tongue."

"The cow tongue?"

"You know—the one Loralee gave us out of her freezer. To make sandwiches for lunch. Mom can't get it thawed out. Loralee said tongue sandwiches are gourmet and so Mom really wants to make them, but she says this one is only fit for a doorstop."

Just then they heard bumping sounds and muffled exclamations. Coasting regally down the narrow wooden stairs from the hay loft on her behind, came Aunt Fan.

Both girls rushed over to her. "Aunt Fan! Are you all right?"

"I just slipped on some loose hay. You shouldn't have loose hay lying about, Quincy. Yes, I'm unharmed, thank you. In fact, I believe the crick in my neck has gone! It's like a miracle!" As she was hoisted upright, Aunt Fan brushed off her robe. "By the way, you've got bats up there, you know."

Bats...but of course! Why didn't I think of that before...

"Come on," cried Quincy. "I think I know where the Bagels are!"

12

A Mind-boggling Thought

When they drew near the house, Quincy suddenly stopped short. "Well, I'll be! Look, there's Dad and Morris. They're playing horseshoes already! They must have found some stakes somewhere."

"They're too close together," yelled Aunt Fan. "The stakes are supposed to be forty feet apart, and that's not forty feet."

The two players did not appear to hear her. "I got a ringer," shouted Morris gleefully. "And Dad hasn't even got one yet!"

"Ha." Mr. Rumpel rubbed his hands together. "Just you wait. I'm just getting warmed up."

Carefully taking up his position, Mr. Rumpel narrowed his eyes and sighted his target. Then he heaved his horseshoe. It land-ed with a clunk beside his last throw—somewhere beyond the stake.

"Let me have those horseshoes," demanded Aunt Fan. She discarded her hot water bottle, camera and binoculars, hitched up her robe and strode over. "I'll show you how we do it back in Ontario."

As Aunt Fan made her third ringer in a row, Quincy said, "We're going to the bat house. I think the Bagels might be there. Are you coming, Morris?"

"Yeah, I guess so," sighed Morris. "This is getting boring. But first I'm going to get some food. I'll meet you guys there."

"Bring us something to eat, too."

Leaving Aunt Fan and Mr. Rumpel engrossed in their game and Morris on his way back to the house, Leah and Quincy set out for the far pasture.

"Why do you think the Bagels are at the bat house?" Leah said, pausing to pick some Queen Anne's lace.

"Because there's nowhere else they could be. They'd probably be fascinated with it. As I said, they seem to be interested in old things."

"The bat house is sure old, all right. And it suits them. It's kind of spooky and they're sort of strange."

"There it is..." Ahead of them, almost hidden in a thicket of ancient aspens and enmeshed in a shroud of creeping blackberry vines and decaying wild roses, was a small log building. The roof had fallen in at one end, and there were gaping black holes where windows had once been. The half-open door creaked eerily as it swung back and forth in the faint breeze.

"I don't think anybody's there," said Leah.

"It's pretty quiet, all right," said Quincy. "But you never know. Just keep out of sight, and *keep quiet*."

Suddenly they heard something crashing through the bushes behind them.

"YO!" hollered a voice.

"Morris, shut up," hissed Quincy. "We're on a stake-out here."

Clutching a plastic Safeway bag, Morris emerged from the underbrush. His face was flushed and sweaty, and his hair stuck to his forehead.

"Guess what?" he gasped. "A dinosaur egg has gone missing from a museum in Alberta! I just heard it on the radio. And that's not all! I think the police are looking for an old Land Rover!"

Leah's eyes went wide. "Like Aunt Fan's?"

"There must be hundreds of them," said Quincy. "Still, Aunt Fan *was* at the Tyrrell Museum. Morris, are you sure about the Land Rover?"

"Pretty sure. Anyway, the Bagels do act kind of weird," said Morris. "And Justin and Dustin both had backpacks on when I saw them in the barn, so they could have been stashing the egg right then!"

Leah frowned. "But why hide it in our barn? It doesn't make sense."

"It might," said Quincy. "If the Bagels really did steal a dinosaur egg and they heard the police were looking for it, they would hide it right away, until the heat was off. Then they'd come back and get it sometime and sell it to a rich private collector——like the Aga Khan, maybe."

"It must be worth zillions!" Morris sank to the ground, quite overwhelmed. Opening his shopping bag, he took out some leftover popadams stuffed with cold spaghetti and dill pickles, and began to eat.

Leah peered into the bag with distaste. "You might at least have brought us some muffins or apples or something."

"You know, things in a museum are really public property," said Quincy. "They belong to all of us. It is simply abominable to steal from a museum!"

Then she had another thought.

"Oh, wow. What about Aunt Fan? If the Bagels really did steal this egg, and Aunt Fan drove the getaway car, the police will be after her, too! She would be an accomplice. This is mind-boggling!"

13

More B and B'ers

Quincy sat down on a nearby log to think things over.

"What will happen to poor Aunt Fan? Do you suppose she'll have to go to jail?" wondered Leah.

Quincy frowned. "I don't think so. Not if she didn't know about the heist. I think we'd better look for this egg. If the Bagels did steal it, they could hide it somewhere around here and no one would suspect. Did the radio say how big it is, Morris?"

"Nope. But it probably wouldn't be a hypselosaurus one. That would be too big to hide. It might be an albertosaurus egg, though. That would fit in a backpack."

"Well, let's get started," said Quincy, jumping up. "The Bagels might be hiding it right this minute! We'll begin by searching the bat house, since we're already here."

"We can't do it now. I forgot to tell you. Mom says she needs you both at home right away. Some more B and B'ers just drove in."

Quincy stopped in her tracks. "More B and B'ers? Good grief! Well, it's up to you then, Morris. You'll have to carry on by yourself. Search the bat house first. Then look thoroughly around Dad's workshop and the old pig pen, and the duck house by the slough."

"It's not fun by myself. Do I have to?"

"Yes. It's very important. You are doing it for the museum, remember. Even for your own children. Even for the whole world!"

Leaving Morris muttering to himself, the two girls ran back to the house.

"This is exciting," said Leah. "I wonder who the new people are?"

"*I* wonder where Mom will put them! We don't have any rooms left. Do you know what I bet, Leah? I bet you and I end up sleeping in the tree house."

"I'm not sleeping in the tree house. With all the spiders and coyotes? No way. Even

Morris wouldn't stay out there last night."

When they got to the kitchen, they found Mrs. Rumpel and Aunt Fan seated at the table, stuffing mushrooms.

"That beef tongue is as tough as an old shoe," said Mrs. Rumpel, as she rammed a mixture of bread crumbs, grated cheese and hard-boiled egg into the limp mushrooms. "We can't possibly serve it, and now we've got these extra people to feed..."

"What kind of people are they?" asked Quincy.

"Aunt Fan thinks they're government birders. They've got cameras and tape recorders, and a cellular phone, even. They were asking what time it gets dark around here, and do we have any spotted owls."

"Spotted owls are an endangered species," said Quincy. "I guess the government is really worried about them. But you're going to need more than stuffed mushrooms for lunch."

"Oh, we are having more. We're going to make open-faced peanut butter and banana sandwiches. I'm going to cut the banana slices into flower shapes and sprinkle the sand-wiches with sunflower seeds. We promised people exquisite meals, and that's what they're going to get. Now I want you girls to move your things out of the attic. We'll need to use your room for the new people."

"What are their names?" asked Quincy.

"They said just to call them Fred and Barney."

Leah eyed her mother suspiciously. "So, if this Fred and Barney get our room in the attic, where are we supposed to go?"

"I thought you wouldn't mind sleeping out in the tree house for one night. It might be fun."

Quincy rolled her eyes. "Mother, it would definitely not be fun. Besides, what about Morris? We're not sleeping in the tree house if he's there, no matter what."

"He can use the hammock on the porch. It's going to be a nice warm night. Now, hurry up—and hurry back down." Mrs. Rumpel waved them away with a mushroom. "Dad is trying to keep the birders busy until lunch is ready. Oh, by the way, did you find the Bagels?"

Quincy shook her head. "Nope."

"I'm wondering if this bed-and-breakfast business is so great," fumed Leah, as the two girls plodded upstairs. "There's so much work to do."

"I'm wondering who these new guys really are! Fred and Barney just have to be phoney names. I mean, did you ever hear of real people called that?"

Up in their attic bedroom, they stripped their beds and gathered up their scattered clothes. Shoving her belongings into her backpack, Quincy heaved it out the window. Then, leaving Leah rounding up her pink pigs, she climbed down the ladder and went on downstairs. A murmur of voices was coming from the living room.

She was just about to peek in when she noticed her mother wildly waving her arms at her from the kitchen.

"Psssst! Psssst! Quincy, come quick! It's Morris!"

14

Government Birders

A swampy smell was wafting in through the screen door.

Standing on the mat outside was Morris. His brown eyes glared accusingly at Quincy from his mud-streaked face. His blonde hair was caked with dirt, and muddy water oozed from his pants and dripped onto the porch.

"Please do something with him," pleaded Mrs. Rumpel. "We just finished making all those dumb sandwiches, and now the new people want breakfast!"

"Oh, well, Mom, *c'est la vie*, I guess." Then Quincy turned to her brother. "What happened to you?"

"I fell in the slough, and it's all your fault."

Prodding Morris ahead of her, Quincy strode out behind the house to the garden hose. Setting him in the flower bed, she turned on the water.

"YOW! You're freezing me! Help! You're going to pay for this, Quincy..."

At that moment, a backpack came hurtling out of the attic window. "Ooops, sorry!" trilled a voice, as Quincy went sprawling.

For a moment she lay there glowering up at the window, but Leah had gone. Quincy gingerly picked herself up from the flattened nasturtiums.

"Well, stop staring," she said to the shivering Morris. "Did you find the egg?"

"There was one in the old duck house. I want to go in now, Quincy. I'm all cold."

"Not yet. This could be very important. Now, tell me. Was it sort of hidden, like as if somebody had hidden it? Was it heavy? Did it look like a fossil?"

"Sort of. Kind of. Maybe, I guess."

"This is very interesting! Where is it now?"

"Gone. Totalled. And man, am I glad! It really stunk when it broke."

"Morris, if it stank, then it wasn't a

dinosaur egg. You know that. It was just an old duck egg."

"I never said it was a dinosaur egg. I just said it kind of looked like a fossil, sort of."

"They don't look like birdwatchers to me," whispered Leah, as she and Quincy carried plates of wobbling stuffed mushrooms, assorted sandwiches, toast, porridge and soft-boiled eggs into the dining room. "Birdwatchers usually wear hats like Aunt Fan's, and sort of rougher clothes."

"Not birdwatchers—government birders. There's a big difference, Aunt Fan says. She says birdwatchers are just ordinary people who watch birds for fun. Birders are more business-like." Narrowing her eyes, Quincy studied the two men in crisp white shirts and sharply pressed pants striding hungrily towards the table. *Dad looks sort of scruffy beside them, even in his good jeans and his giant silver belt buckle. And he seems shorter, somehow.*

Just as they were about to sit down, there was a sudden commotion at the front door. In straggled the four Bagels, accompanied by some chickens and goats, and Snowflake. Mrs. Bagel's shiny green legs were stuck all over with feathers, and Mr. Bagel had a hole in the seat of his green pants. Only one of the twins wore a baseball cap.

"Oh, there you are," said Mrs. Rumpel. "You're just in time. Did you have a nice walk?" Turning to Quincy, she muttered, "Get those animals out of here!"

"We did not have a nice walk," said Mrs. Bagel. "Poor Justin lost his cap, and Dustin's tooth came out. The goats or the chickens must have eaten them. Those dreadful creatures followed us everywhere."

"It was boring," said Justin. "Except for the bat. *That* was sort of interesting. But of course bats are not active in the daytime, so it was just hanging around."

"Boy, that wath a really old houth." Dustin was spitting through the gap in his front teeth.

"He means the duck house," said Mrs. Bagel quickly.

"No, I don't. I mean the houth with the big bokth."

Mr. Bagel cleared his throat. "Never mind. The prospect of another delightful meal brightened our otherwise dull and uneventful morning."

"Have a mushroom," said Mrs. Rumpel, passing the platter. "They're still nice and hot."

"They've only got peanut butter and banana sandwiches," complained Justin. "With no lids."

"You're lucky," said Morris. "You almost got boiled tongue." Now freshly dressed and engaged as a busboy, he hovered behind the diners, impatiently waiting to clear the dishes.

As Quincy and Leah prepared to serve Mrs. Rumpel's specialty dessert with soup spoons (the Pineapple Ambrosia being not quite set), Quincy wiggled her eyebrows at her sister and murmured something.

Leah looked puzzled. "What? I can't hear you. You're talking out of the side of your mouth."

"I said, watch 'em. Watch the new guys—Fred and Barney!"

When she returned from her next trip to the dining room, Leah was beaming. "I think they were looking at my moose picture! It's probably better than I thought. Maybe I should put a *For Sale* sticker on it."

"Not that! I mean, notice how they're always watching the Bagels. Leah, I don't believe they're government birders at all. Why, they weren't even interested in Aunt Fan's quail! You know what I think? I think they're Mounties in plain clothes, and Fred and Barney are their aliases."

"But what are they doing here?"

"They've tracked the dinosaur egg here, of course."

"Wow. How did you figure all that out?"

"Well, mostly it's their moustaches. Then there's the way they suddenly arrived here with no notice or anything. And it's also how they're dressed, all sort of neat and crisp. And the way they keep watching the Bagels makes me sure they're here to find the dinosaur egg."

"Wow."

"What are you talking about?" asked Morris, garnishing a peanut butter sandwich with some pickles from the pickle dish.

"Tell you later," said Quincy. "Just keep your eyes on everybody, especially the two new guys."

"Fred and Barney? They're neat. They're going to teach me to arm-wrestle." Morris held up his arm, flexing his muscle hopefully.

Quincy looked at Leah. "What did I tell you? I'll bet all Mounties arm-wrestle. They probably do it in their training course."

15

Moustaches

The rest of the afternoon was uneventful. Having declined a game of horseshoes, the four Bagels moved out to the verandah to play Scrabble among themselves, under the watchful eyes of Leah and Quincy.

"Would you look at that," whispered Quincy. "Justin is trying to use *batmobiling*, and they're letting him get away with it!"

Fred and Barney also settled on the verandah to read old magazines, after a sightseeing tour of the premises, a game of horseshoes and an arm-wrestling session with Morris.

"Everybody seems to be enjoying themselves," Mr. Rumpel said happily to his wife, as he gazed out the window at the relaxing guests. "And it seems our old buildings are a real hit! I guess we could almost call them heritage buildings in our next brochure.

What do you think?"

"I suppose so," said Mrs. Rumpel, as she thumbed through a cookbook. "What do you think about tofu and spinach croquettes with parsley sauce and potatoes au gratin for dinner tonight?"

"Sure. Sounds fine."

"Or maybe not. Maybe we should have Tangy Tofu Tacos. Or would they be better for lunch tomorrow...Still, I do have quite a lot of tofu to use up. I don't know why Quincy bought so much. And then there are all those eggplants..."

Just then Leah flitted past, on her way to get some snacks from the fridge.

"Still, I can't help but wonder what attracts everybody to those old buildings..." went on Mrs. Rumpel. In the kitchen, Leah pricked up her ears.

"Mr. Bagel tells me they own an art shop near Vancouver, so they'd probably be interested in historical ruins and other items of culture," said Mr. Rumpel.

Clutching some plastic containers, Leah

hustled back to Quincy with this new information.

Quincy was not impressed. "Just because they have an art gallery doesn't mean they can't be involved in a dinosaur egg heist."

"But maybe that's why they keep looking at my moose! They probably want to buy it for their gallery."

Growing bored with watching their inert suspects, the two girls took off to the privacy of the tree house. Sitting cross-legged on her sleeping bag, Quincy inspected Leah's selection of snacks. "Oh, good, you found some Pineapple Ambrosia." Opening the margarine tub, she prepared to take a happy mouthful. "Ugh! What's this green stuff?" she cried.

"I was in a hurry," said Leah, poking the slimy contents with her spoon. "It might be spinach. Or maybe not. What a bummer! Oh, well, we've still got a few stuffed mushrooms and some carrots and cold pancakes."

Quincy popped a mushroom into her mouth. "They're not so good cold," she said.

"Now, getting back to our problem. The way I figure it, the Bagels definitely look guilty. Did you see the way they hedged around about going to the bat house? I think either they've already hidden the egg, or they are just about to. They sure won't want to be caught with it in their possession, now that the Mounties have shown up."

Leah frowned. "But the art gallery..."

"It could be a front for a big crime ring. Or maybe not. Maybe the art business isn't too good right now and this egg was just sitting there waiting to be heisted and the Bagels thought it might as well be them. You know, sort of a case of *carpe diem*."

"What?"

"Leah, you have to start reading more. It means 'seize the day.' It's Italian, or something. So, anyway, if we could find the egg before the Mounties do, we could get the Bagels to give it back and turn themselves in."

"But that's awful. Then they'd go to jail, and it would be all our fault. Maybe Dustin and Justin would end up like orphans!"

For a moment Quincy was silent. Finally she said, "Maybe you're right. Maybe we'd better just say we found the egg, which would be true. If we find it. But then, if it's a crime ring, they shouldn't really get away with it, should they? Especially stealing from a museum. But then there's Aunt Fan. It would be awful it we got her in trouble when all she did was drive the car! Leah, we are in a real moral dilemma. I've never been in a real moral dilemma before."

Leah nodded while Quincy thought some more. Finally she spoke.

"We'll do it! Here's the plan. We wait until dark—maybe even after everybody's gone to bed. Then we go into action."

"What kind of action?"

"We begin our real search for the missing dinosaur egg!"

"Why do we have to wait till dark?"

"Because we don't want to be seen, of course. And anyway, that gives the Bagels plenty of time to hide it—if they haven't done it already. So then we find it and bring it up here."

"And then what?"

"Then I'll decide what to do next."

"I don't want to go to the bat house at night, Quince."

"It will be all right. We'll take flashlights and Snowflake and Mor—Leah, did you hear somebody hollering just now?"

"It's Mom. I think she wants us back at the house. Something about Aunt Fan..."

16

A Horrible Thought

In the kitchen they were greeted by Morris, who held up one arm. "Look, my muscle's bigger already. I've been practising."

Mrs. Rumpel sat at the table, which was strewn with cookbooks. Her glasses had slid down her nose, and her hair stuck out in all directions.

"I need some new cookbooks," said Mrs. Rumpel. "Quincy, I'm worried about Aunt Fan. She hasn't been acting herself lately. And now she's gone out alone somewhere, even though she's got that crick in her neck. She says it's better, but I know it isn't. I think you girls had better go and look for her."

"We will, Mom," said Quincy. "Did she take anything with her?"

"I think she had her knitting bag. That's funny, isn't it? Why would she take her knitting bag? When I asked her where she was going, she just said, *Ask me no questions and I'll tell you no lies*."

"That doesn't sound like Aunt Fan," said Leah.

"You're right," said Quincy. "It doesn't. We'd better find her right away."

"Wait a minute," said Mrs. Rumpel. "What *am* I going to make for dinner? Maybe I should do something with those twelve eggplants you bought the other day, Quincy. Why on earth *did* you buy so many?"

"I dunno. They just looked so beautiful— all purple and shiny. Don't worry, Mom. You'll think of something..."

"Doesn't anybody want to arm-wrestle with me?" whined Morris.

"Get Justin or Dustin," said Quincy, pushing open the back door.

"I did, but they've got awfully big arms."

"Ha. They beat him, is what he means!"

When they got outside, Leah said, "Aunt Fan is acting really strange, isn't she?"

Quincy's face was solemn. "More than

strange. I've just had a horrible thought! What if she *is* involved in the heist? What if it's not the Bagels at all? What if *Aunt Fan* took the egg?"

"Oh, no!"

Quincy nodded. "Remember when I found her stuck in the blackberries this morning? Was she really just following the quail, or was she looking for a hiding place for the egg? And in the barn. Why did she go up in the loft by herself? Was she trying to hide it up there? What other reason could there be? And, after all, it was *her* Land Rover that drove here from the museum. We've got to find her, Leah!"

They found Aunt Fan sitting on a cushion by the rock pile.

"Mom was worried about you, Aunt Fan," cried Quincy. "What are you doing out here?"

"What does it look like I'm doing, girl? I'm getting away from your mother. I love her dearly, but she was driving me bananas with her tofu nonsense."

"I know what you mean," said Leah, sitting down on the rock pile beside her great-aunt. After a few minutes, she got up, rubbing her behind. "I see why you brought the cushion, Aunt Fan."

"So that's what you had in your knitting bag!" cried Quincy.

"That and my binoculars and camera and bird book. What did you suppose I had?"

"Um, nothing special. Aunt Fan, I have to know one more thing. What were you doing up in the hay loft this morning?"

"Hoping to see some baby owls, of course. The nests are usually high up in old barns, you know."

"Of course," said Quincy in a small voice. "I knew that."

17

The Game

At dinner that night, Mrs. Rumpel surprised everyone, even herself, by coming up with a delicious tofu and eggplant casserole.

"Oh, ratatouille!" said Justin. "We haven't had that since we were in France."

"It'th not quite the thame," said Dustin. "But it'th thtill pretty tathty."

When everyone had been fed and the dishes cleaned up, the kitchen table was taken over by Morris and his Monopoly board. He arranged the houses and hotels in neat rows and sorted the play money into denominations.

"Want to play?" he asked the twins, as he riffled through the hundred-dollar bills.

"We usually play Scrabble."

"Boring!" Morris shook the dice enticingly.

"Justin and Dustin don't play games of chance," said Mrs. Bagel. "Why don't you

boys show Morris how to play Brain Quest?"
But Justin and Dustin were eyeing the stacks
of Monopoly money with growing interest.

"It lookth like fun," said Dustin.

"It is. See, I give you all this money to start
with. You can pretend it's real, and then you
buy things."

"Oh, boy!" said Justin. "I want to buy the
railroads!"

Meanwhile, Quincy began organizing the
evening's operation. "I'll get our equipment
together," she told Leah. "You get some cook-
ies or something in case we get hungry."

She was in the utility room hooking flashlights onto her belt when Leah found her.

"What did you get?" asked Quincy.

Leah pulled a package of fig bars out of her
shirtfront. "I didn't want the twins to see,"
she explained. "They're in the kitchen with
Morris. He's teaching them to play
Monopoly. I think he's cleaning up on them."

"That figures. Justin and Dustin don't
stand a chance. Tell Morris to come to the tree

house, *stat*. We have to talk. But don't let the twins know. This operation has to be kept absolutely secret."

"Morris won't want to come when he's winning."

"Leah, it's getting dark. Make him come. It will soon be time for us to make our move. I'll keep my eye on the Bagels and the Mounties, to make sure they don't give us the slip. I'll meet you in the tree house in a few minutes."

As Quincy stalked through the house checking on its occupants, she was satisfied to see that everyone was reasonably settled. Mr. Rumpel and Mr. Bagel seemed to have dozed off watching the news on TV, while Mrs. Bagel was absorbed in putting silver-coloured polish on her fingernails. Mrs. Rumpel had retired early with a pile of cookbooks. Aunt Fan was soaking in the bathtub.

Ha, thought Quincy, looking at the two figures in the corner of the living room, hunched over a checker board, *I didn't think Fred and Barney would let the Bagels out of their sight for long!*

Suddenly the evening quiet was shattered by piercing shrieks, and Justin and Dustin came hurtling out of the kitchen. "Ma! Morris took all our money!"

Everyone snapped to attention.

"Did somebody say something about money?" asked Mr. Bagel, waking up with a start.

"Where is he?" screeched Mrs. Bagel, knocking over her bottle of nail polish as she leaped up from the chesterfield.

Fred and Barney stopped their game and stared as Morris, shedding hundred-dollar bills, streaked through the house and out the front door, pursued by Mrs. Bagel.

"What's the matter?" cried Mrs. Rumpel, running down the stairs in her dressing gown.

"Did something happen to Morris?" asked Aunt Fan, appearing at the top of the stairs in a striped bath towel and orange shower cap.

"Not yet," said Mr. Rumpel.

"That son of yours is a thief!" Mrs. Bagel shook her fist at Mrs. Rumpel. "He took our munchkins' money!"

Mrs. Rumpel's eyes flashed dangerously. She shoved out her chin and folded her arms across her chest. "Say that again. I double dare you to say that again…"

"Whoa! Just a minute, everybody," said Quincy. "The kids were playing Monopoly, and Morris was probably winning." She turned to the twins. "Isn't that right? He won all your Monopoly money, didn't he?"

The twins shrugged. "It's a dumb game, anyway," said Justin. "It's an NSR game."

"What's that?"

"No Skill Required."

After this skirmish, Justin and Dustin were marched off to bed by their mother. Mrs. Rumpel returned to her quarters, Aunt Fan to her bath, and the checkers players to their game.

Leaving her father and Mr. Bagel disagreeing over whether to watch the hockey game or a nature show about the life cycle of the water beetle, Quincy finally took off for the tree house.

18

Flashlights and Fig Bars

When she reached the top of the ladder and looked inside the tree house, Quincy's mouth fell open in surprise.

An old lace curtain hung by thumbtacks across the open window. Between the two sleeping bags was a pink bathmat, and on a cardboard box spread with a flowered silk scarf, six pink plastic pigs were tastefully arranged beside a jar of nasturtiums and the package of fig bars.

Leah was beaming. "How do you like it? I think it's much homier now."

"It's awful. I can't stand it," said Morris. He was sitting cross-legged on Quincy's sleeping bag, counting Monopoly money. "What are the flashlights for?"

"First, we make sure everyone in the house has gone to bed. We'll wait for the lights to go out. Then we go down to the bat house and *really* search for that dinosaur egg."

"What do we do with it if we find it?" wondered Leah. "And what about Aunt Fan?"

"I'm sure she had nothing to do with the egg. All she thinks about is her birdwatching. First thing in the morning, we will make contact with the Bagels. We will tell them we have the egg and ask them what they want to do about it. After that it won't be our moral dilemma any more. It will be theirs."

"Well, just so long as I don't have to go in the bat house at midnight," said Leah. "I don't think I could stand that."

"Leah, there's nothing special about midnight. Anyway, I guarantee we'll go the minute the lights in the house go out and we know everybody has gone to bed. Now, turn off your dumb flashlights, both of you, or your batteries will go dead."

"I wish you wouldn't talk about going dead," said Leah.

"When do we get to eat the fig bars?" asked Morris, flicking his flashlight on and off.

"I told you. Later. Now turn that thing off!"

For a while they sat there in the dark, watching the house through their lace-curtained window.

Finally Leah yawned. "I don't think they're *ever* going to bed. I'm going to lie down for a minute. You guys can watch."

Morris was the next to give up his vigil. After ten minutes of listening to his noisy yawns, Quincy dismissed him from his post, and he sagged down gratefully in a heap on the bathmat.

For a while Quincy kept watch as the lights of Rumpel Ranch went out one by one. At last only one light remained—Aunt Fan's, in the living room.

Leah was snoring softly, and Morris was mumbling in his sleep, "Gimme Park Place and Boardwalk. Gimme Park Place and Boardwalk..."

In a nearby tree an owl hooted. Quincy shivered. Pulling her sleeping bag up around her, she propped herself against the wall and closed her eyes.

When she woke up and looked out, the house was completely dark. She shook Morris and Leah awake.

"Come on, guys, it's time to go."

Leah sat up slowly, rubbing her eyes. "Go where?"

"On our mission—our mission for the museum. The dinosaur egg."

"Egg?" muttered Morris. "Is it breakfast time? I could eat an egg. And some bacon...pancakes."

"Morris, wake up. Now, come on every-body—down the ladder, and don't forget your flashlights."

19

The Bat House

As the three circles of light wobbled across the back field, a ghostly white shape followed them.

"Here comes good old Snowflake, our trusty companion," said Morris.

"He looks sort of sleepy," said Leah, who was wearing a woollen toque pulled down over her ears. "He's not used to getting up at night. What time is it, anyway?"

"Shhhh!" Quincy held her finger up to her lips. "I think it's kind of late. We all fell asleep. Leah, why are you wearing your toque?"

"I feel safer in it. Kind of late? How late?"

Quincy shone the flashlight on her watch. "Sort of like around twelve, I guess."

"Like exactly midnight!" said Morris, peeking over her arm.

Leah stopped in her tracks. "Then I'm going back. I will not go into the bat house at midnight."

"But the egg," pleaded Quincy. "Aren't you going to help find the egg for the museum? We might even get our pictures in the paper."

Slowly, Leah began to move forward again. "Well, I guess I'll come. But I'm not staying long."

The moon was low in the sky now, and the shadows long. They trudged on in silence until Leah cried out, "Ouch! Ouch! You stepped on my heel, Morris. Back up!"

"I couldn't help it. My flashlight went off. I think the battery is dead. Quincy, have you got any more batteries?"

"N.O. I *told* you not to keep turning it on and off."

"I've never been here at night," said Leah. "It seems an awful lot farther. And my heel hurts. I hope the museum appreciates us doing this."

"Maybe we'll get a reward." The more

excited he got, the squeakier Morris's voice became. "Thousands and thousands of big ones!"

"Keep your voice down," ordered Quincy. "Just in case somebody is around. We're getting close now."

The little group stumbled on. Now they were past the barn, past Aunt Fan's rock pile, and through the far pasture.

At last they reached the bat house. Except for the rustle of the quivering aspens around it, the old homestead cabin was wrapped in shadows and silence.

"There's no light," said Quincy. "Nobody's here."

As she pushed open the sagging door, there was a scrabbling sound inside.

"Mice," said Morris.

"MICE?!!" Leah grabbed Quincy with both hands, dropping her flashlight. It promptly went out.

"Now you've done it," said Quincy. "Now we've only got one."

As they shuffled inside, something

swished by over their heads and out the open door.

"A bat!" Releasing her grip on Quincy, Leah yanked her toque down over her face.

"Probably just a bird." Quincy tried to sound reassuring, but her voice was shaky.

"No way," said Morris. "That wasn't a bird. It didn't have any feathers. It was a bat, all right."

Leah sagged against her sister. "I think I'm going to faint..."

"No, you're not. Now come on, everybody, let's find that egg!"

But there were only two rooms, and as they shone their single light around, they saw that there weren't many places to search. There was a rough wooden counter and some shelves, some broken furniture, and a wooden crate.

Quincy shone the beam of her flashlight into the crate. "Huh. No dinosaur egg in here. Just some pieces of wood. Quel disappointment!"

"Those are pieces of old picture frames," said Leah.

"I see some old rusty coffee tins on the shelf," said Morris. "And an *egg* carton! Get it down, Quincy."

Could it be? Would they hide a dinosaur egg in an egg carton? Maybe that would be the safest place. Who would ever look in there? She reached up and got the carton.

"I think there's something in here," she said. Leah and Morris hung expectantly over her shoulder as she carefully lifted the lid.

"Baby mice!" shouted Morris. "A whole nest of pink baby mice! Oh, boy, this is my lucky day!"

"You're not going to keep them," said Quincy. "Put them back. Come on, we have to check out the back room."

As the solitary beam swept around the bare room, Leah cried, "Eyes! Eyes!" and pointed to a small huddled shape in the corner. "It's a ...it's a ...whatchamacallit!"

Reflecting the light were two button-eyes in a small masked face.

Morris was elated. "It's a little raccoon! This place is full of animal babies!"

"And we'd better not disturb this one," said Quincy. "Its mother may not be so friendly. Anyway, I'm sure the egg isn't here. Who wants to search the barn?"

"Now?" chorused Leah and Morris. "No way!"

They were on their way back to the main room when Morris said, "Whoops, I just kicked something." Bending down, he picked up a wad of blue cloth. "It's Justin's baseball cap—and there's bubblegum stuck inside it!"

"I guess the goats didn't eat it after all," said Leah.

"And they didn't eat Dustin's tooth, either," said Morris. "See, it's stuck in the middle of the gum."

"How revolting," said Quincy. "Let's go home."

20

Something Strange

The disheartened and weary investigators stumbled homewards. As they got near the house, Morris cried out, "Look, it's all lit up!"

"I don't believe it," said Quincy. "Everybody was asleep when we left. What's going on?"

For Rumpel Ranch was ablaze with lights. Bumping into each other in their haste, the investigators hurried on.

When they reached the front porch, they stood with their noses pressed against the window, looking in. "Everybody's milling around in there," said Leah. "I see Mom and Dad, and there's Aunt Fan, eating something..."

"I see the Bagels," said Morris. "But Mrs. Bagel looks sort of funny. Dustin and Justin are eating something, too. It looks like choco-late cake. It *is* chocolate cake! *Everybody's got chocolate cake!"*

"Mrs. Bagel has got kind of a mud pack on her face," said Quincy. "There are the Mounties in the dining room. One of them is writing something in a little book..."

"Everybody is in their pyjamas," said Morris. "They're having a pyjama party, and we're not there!"

"Don't worry, we soon will be." Turning the doorknob, Quincy pushed against the door. It wouldn't open.

"We're locked out!"

They rattled the knob and thumped the door, and at last Mrs. Rumpel heard them.

"Why, it's Quincy, Leah and Morris!" she exclaimed, as her wan and hollow-eyed off-spring stumbled in. "I thought you three were asleep."

"We've been at the bat house," said Morris. "Where's the chocolate cake?"

"What is everybody doing up?" asked Quincy.

It turned out that Mr. and Mrs. Rumpel had heard a noise downstairs and had gone down to investigate.

Aunt Fan, sleeping on the chesterfield, was also awakened by strange sounds. Brandishing Grandpa Rumpel's cane and clad in her MacGregor dressing gown and Indian moccasins, she had sneaked into the dining room.

When they discovered all their house guests assembled in front of Leah's moose picture, Mrs. Rumpel had hospitably brought forth from her freezer a chocolate cake.

"I just wanted to have another look at this in private," Mr. Bagel was saying, nodding towards the painting. "Then everybody else showed up."

But his wife was staring at Morris. "I am wondering what you children were doing at that dreadful old place at this time of night!"

Just look at her, Quincy said to herself. *How she's narrowing her eyes so suspiciously*. She looked at Mrs. Bagel meaningfully. "I think you know why."

Mr. and Mrs. Bagel glanced at one another.

"It starts with an 'E'," said Morris, wiggling his eyebrows.

"The egg," blurted out Leah. "The dinosaur egg!"

Mr. and Mrs. Rumpel looked at her blankly. So did everyone else.

This is not turning out right, thought Quincy. *It's all wrong. I will have to use all my investigator's technique to get to the bottom of this.*

Watching the Bagels shrewdly, she asked, "You mean you are not, and have never been, involved with the dinosaur egg disappearance?"

Mr. Bagel sighed and shook his head. "I guess you'll have to find out sooner or later..."

Aha! thought Quincy.

"We're here about the picture, of course. The missing Modigliani. When we met your Aunt Fan on the cruise, she mentioned an interesting old painting she had seen somewhere on your establishment and, being art dealers, we were intrigued."

"I didn't think it was interesting at all,"

protested Aunt Fan. "I thought it was an ugly picture."

"So it was the Modigliani you were after," said Fred. "We thought so. Did you find it?"

"Don't tell them!" yelled Mrs. Bagel.

"They're Mounties," said Quincy. "You have to tell them."

"They've been trailing us all the way from Alberta," said Mr. Bagel. "But they're not Mounties. I suspect they're art dealers, like us."

"That is true," said Barney. "We heard your little boys talking about finding a lost Modigliani back in the museum in Alberta. So we followed you here. We really want that painting, and we're prepared to pay handsomely for it."

"I didn't think they were birders," muttered Aunt Fan. And she went out to the kitchen to make a pot of tea.

"I never knew we had any valuable old paintings around here," said Mrs. Rumpel.

"I don't think you have, ma'am," said Mr. Bagel. "We've gone over every inch of your buildings, but we couldn't find it. This picture of the moose, or whatever, is the right size, but that's all."

"There used to be an old picture in the crate at the bat house," said Quincy. "It had a sort of weird-looking person with a long greenish face."

"That's it!" Mrs. Bagel's own face was pink with excitement. "That's the missing Modigliani! WHERE IS IT?"

Leah pointed to her moose painting, hanging on the wall.

Mrs. Bagel began to choke. "You mean you painted over it?"

"I thought there was something strange about that picture all along," said Mr. Bagel sadly.

21

No More All-Day Breakfasts

By this time people were really hungry, so Mrs. Rumpel went out to the kitchen to whip up something to eat. When it turned out to be plain scrambled eggs and toast and everyone was quite delighted, she seemed surprised.

"I'm sure we couldn't face one of your fancy-dancy concoctions at this hour, dear," Aunt Fan told her. "Scrambled eggs are just right."

Bright and early the next morning, Fred and Barney took off in their white 4-wheel drive.

"They didn't even wait for breakfast," said Mrs. Rumpel. "And I was thinking about making eggs Benedict on toasted English muffins with codfish balls...what did you say, Quincy?"

"I just said they sure looked like Mounties."

"Who, dear?"

"Fred and Barney, of course. Or whoever they really are."

"You don't have to snap at me like that, young lady."

"She's just mad because she was wrong about everything," said Leah.

Mr. Rumpel pulled a piece of paper from his pocket. "Their cheque is stamped *Frederick and Barnwhistle, Dealers in Fine Art.*"

"I wasn't wrong about everything," said Quincy. "I said Fred and Barney were phoney names, and they were."

"By the way," said Mr. Rumpel, "I heard on the late news last night that the missing dinosaur egg was not really missing after all. It had just been put in the wrong display case at the museum."

"Imagine that," said Mrs. Rumpel.

"I might have known," groaned Quincy. "That's the last time I listen to Morris."

◆

Aunt Fan bought Leah's moose painting for a modest sum. There was no way it could ever be restored, said the Bagels, due to the paint remover she had used. But Aunt Fan didn't care. "I like it the way it is," she said.

As the five Rumpels stood on the front verandah waving good-bye to the last of their guests, Mrs. Rumpel asked Morris, "What was in the brown paper bag you gave Justin just now?"

"His baseball cap. We found it."

"That was nice of you, dear. Look, he's putting it on. Now he's taking it off. No, he isn't. It doesn't seem to be coming off..."

"I think I hear the phone!" said Morris, suddenly bolting into the house.

Mr. Rumpel grinned at his wife. "More customers! I told you this bed-and-breakfast business would be a little gold mine."

A glazed look came over Mrs. Rumpel's face. "Do you realize I haven't been out of the kitchen in *days*? I think we're going to take 'exquisite meals' and 'all-day breakfast' off

116

our advertising from now on."

"Way to go, Mom," said Quincy. "And no exciting trail rides...except, of course, we *could* get some more horses. There's another horse auction coming up really soon."

Mrs. Rumpel did not look impressed.

Quincy turned to Leah. "Come on, let's move back into our room. I'm looking forward to a good night's sleep in my own bed tonight, now that my moral dilemma is over."

"Me, too," said Leah. "I've just been through a very traumatic experience, you know, selling my moose picture. It's sort of like selling one's child, I imagine. Of course, the fifty dollars helps."

Just then they heard a whoop from the house, and Morris came rushing out. "Guess what?" he cried. "A whole bunch more B and B'ers are coming! They'll be here for lunch."

"Who is it, and how many this time?" quavered Mrs. Rumpel, looking pale.

Morris frowned in concentration. "I sort of forget. He sounded kind of French, though. I think he said he was a minister—or something. Maybe it was a prime minister. Oh, yes. Now I remember. There are six of them. Or did he say sixteen..."

Quincy Rumpel and the Sasquatch
of Phantom Cove

When the Rumpels visit their dear friends Bert and
Ernie at their new fishing resort, things are not
quite as expected. There are no fish, and they find
signs of a creature that looks a lot like a sasquatch!

Morris Rumpel and the Wings of Icarus

Morris's summer vacation with his grandparents
holds more adventure than even he has bargained
for. And why is he being followed by the mysteri-
ous, icicle-eyed stranger?

Quincy Rumpel and the Woolly Chaps

The Rumpel family has just moved to their grandparents' ranch in Cranberry Corners, and Quincy is
determined to buy a horse. So she sets out to earn
the money by working as a ranch nanny.

Quincy Rumpel and the Mystifying Experience

A trip to Ontario for Great-grandmother Twistle's
ninety-first birthday doesn't work out as planned.
When they arrive, it seems that Great-grandma
Twistle has disappeared!